Johnny's Big Idea

By Nancy Savage

Illustrations by Amana Yamisha

Whether you have support or not, continue to follow your path and dreams. Eventually, success and support follow.

~ Nancy

Johnny's eyes pop open on Saturday morning as the haze from his dreams fade. Today is the day he is going to see the new *Spider Fang 3D* movie. Johnny and his friends from the neighborhood have been waiting for weeks to see this movie.

Johnny leaps from his bed, tosses his pajamas onto the cluttered floor, and pulls on his favorite t-shirt and jeans. He runs downstairs as fast as his eight-year-old legs can carry him.

"Mom! Let's go see the *Spider Fang* movie now."

Johnny's mom turns from the pile of laundry she is folding and replies, "Only after I finish all the housework, honey. You know that Saturday is cleaning day."

Little Johnny's mind starts to think of ways to help with his mom's eyes brighten at the idea. "What if I help you? Then can we go?"

"Yes, Johnny. If you help me finish cleaning, we can go to the movie." She heads towards her office and calls over her shoulder, "Give me a few minutes to make you a list."

Once the list is complete, Mom opens her wallet. She removes three crisp dollar bills and then fishes out eight quarters.

She enters Johnny's bedroom and hands him the chore list. He reads each numbered item and then she asks, "Do you have any questions?"

"No Mom," Johnny answers. "But if I do, I will ask."

Johnny gets to work.

1. MAKE BED AND CLEAN ROOM

Too easy, Johnny thinks excitedly.

He starts by picking up all the trucks and plastic animals that litter the carpet. Once the toys have been returned to their place, he picks up the clothes that were scattered around the room.

He notices the pj's he had thrown on the floor this morning. Picking them up, he rolls them into a ball and heads for the closet.

Johnny slam dunks them into the hamper. SWOOSH!

"Nothing but net!" he shouts.

He then grabs the comforter off his bed, fluffs it into the air and *SWISH!* It falls around his small shoulders like a cape. From within the folds of the comforter, a green piece of paper floats to the ground and lands with a whisper.

"A dollar!"

Johnny dives for the bill. He stuffs it into the pocket of his jeans and turns back to his list.

2. DUST LIVING ROOM AND FLUFF SOFA CUSHIONS

Picture frames, figurines, and lamps - nothing was forgotten. As Johnny lifts the last object to be cleaned, he finds another fresh dollar bill. "Wow, I'm going to be rich!"

Focusing back on the shortening list, he remembers the couch cushions. The boy marches over to the sofa.

"Abra Kadabra!" With his magical words, Johnny flips the sofa cushions. There, underneath, like two pairs of bright shining eyes, sat four quarters. He adds them to the growing collection in his pocket.

"Dusting and cushions - CHECK!" Johnny barks in a military voice.

3. COLLECT ALL THE TRASH

Johnny strolls to the trash can with his hands stuffed into his pockets, and he eyeballs his prey. "Freeze, trash can!!" Within minutes, Sheriff Johnny has rounded up "criminals" hiding in the garbage. "Come out with your trash up." Johnny tries to control a giggle.

Johnny sees a piece of trash in the can that didn't make it into the bag. When he reaches deep down to pick it up, he realizes it wasn't trash, but..."A dollar!" This is a reward for a job well done.

4. WASH THE DISHES

Johnny peers into the kitchen sink and finds the dishes soaking in a fluffy cloud of suds. He rushes to get a chair and climbs into position.

Johnny waves his hand into the fading bubbles and pulls out the plug. Soapy water swirls down the drain. At the bottom of the sink, four clean quarters lay waiting to be retrieved.

"I'm already up to five dollars!" Johnny shrieks.

"Guess what, Mom?!" he shouts as he comes running into her bedroom.

"What, munchkin?"

"I have finished all but one thing on the list. The last one says **RECYCLE**. How do I do that?" The puzzled helper was eager to complete his list.

"Please collect the recycle bags and bring them to the car. Make sure the bags do not leak," Johnny's mom instructs as she finishes folding the last of the laundry. Johnny dashes out to the garage and gathers the various recycling containers.

As Johnny carries the many bags of recyclables to the trunk of his mother's car, Nan and Jim roll up on their bikes.

"Hey, Johnny, let's ride down to the creek and catch frogs," Jim invites.

Although tempted by the offer, Johnny says, "Can't right now, guys. I am helping my mom with chores. I've already earned five bucks!" The pride spreads across his freckled face. "Then we are going to see *Spider Fang 3D!*"

Johnny says goodbye to his friends, and Jim and Nan ride away wondering what they could do to earn money.

When he returns inside, Johnny discovers his mom is done and waiting to go. "Are you ready, my love?"

"Yes, ma'am!" he exclaims. "But what are we going to do with the recycling?"

"You'll see..." his mother replies mysteriously.

As they head towards the shopping center, Johnny excitedly tells the events of the day. "Five bucks, Mom! Can you believe that?"

Johnny's mom grins, taking her eyes off the boy in the rearview mirror. She pulls into the recycling center.

"Giddy up, Johnny," his mother says.

They climb out of the car and remove the bags from the trunk. Each carrying their load, they shuffle up to the recycling machine. Once each of the bags were empty, the machine adds up a total of $6.45.

Mom tells Johnny to close his eyes and hold out his hand. She then removes the ticket from the machine and places it into Johnny's open hand. "This is for you, kiddo. Thanks for all your help today. You can buy candy and popcorn if you would like, or you can save it for your piggy bank."

"Thanks, Mom! It was my pleasure!" replies Johnny.

They make their way over to the movie theater after they cash in Johnny's recycling reward. His mom steps up to the ticket counter and says, "One adult and one child for the five o'clock showing of *Spider Fang 3D*, please. Thank you!"

Johnny stands by his mother, drooling as he stares at the counter of the snack bar.

He studies each item inside the sparkling clean glass counter.

Johnny finally narrows down his choice.

"I would like the kid's pack, please."

He decides to only spend some of the money and wants to save the rest for his piggy bank. He also decides that $11.45 is not too shabby for the day's work.

"Thank you for helping me today, Johnny. I am happy you decided to save some of your money."

"You are welcome, Mom. Not a bad day's work, huh?" Johnny declares to his mom, while in his mind he thinks, *I should help more often.*

Just after finding the perfect seats, the lights slowly dim. The movie lights up the screen.

Johnny and his mom cuddle up and prepare to watch the movie.

Also by this author
(available on Amazon)

Sweet Bakers Money Makers (The Treasure Hill Series: Children's Stories on Money, Business, Savings, and Entrepreneurship for Kids)

Jim and Nan are assigned a group project: Write a plan for a business you would like to have or open when you grow up. The kids have a neighborhood garage sale coming up and decide to take it one step further and turn their idea into a money making one! They open a lemonade and cupcakes stand. See what happens next. You never know what's in store for you or happening in Treasure Hill!

Made in the USA
Las Vegas, NV
05 July 2022

51143960R00019